Marilyn/God

by Rosary Hartel O'Neill

SAMUEL FRENCH

FOUNDED 1830

NEW YORK HOLLYWOOD LONDON TORONTO

SAMUELFRENCH.COM

MUSIC USE NOTE

Licensees are solely responsible for obtaining formal written permission from copyright owners to use copyrighted music in the performance of this play and are strongly cautioned to do so. If no such permission is obtained by the licensee, then the licensee must use only original music that the licensee owns and controls. Licensees are solely responsible and liable for all music clearances and shall indemnify the copyright owners of the play and their licensing agent, Samuel French, Inc., against any costs, expenses, losses and liabilities arising from the use of music by licensees.

IMPORTANT BILLING AND CREDIT
REQUIREMENTS

All producers of *MARILYN/GOD must* give credit to the Author of the Play in all programs distributed in connection with performances of the Play, and in all instances in which the title of the Play appears for the purposes of advertising, publicizing or otherwise exploiting the Play and/or a production. The name of the Author *must* appear on a separate line on which no other name appears, immediately following the title and *must* appear in size of type not less than fifty percent of the size of the title type.

CHARACTERS

MARILYN MONROE – A movie star, 36. Dressed in a fluid, cream-colored, silk gown slit to the thigh, sandal heels. She looks tattered.

VOICE and **AGENT** – Marilyn's Judges. Are offstage for the course of the play.

SETTING

The action takes place in the mind of Marilyn on an empty stage with a chair.

TIME

Some time between 7:30 pm August 4th and 3:30 am August 5th, 1962, during Marilyn's final hours.

Scene One

*(**SETTING**: We're on an empty stage, in a space of limbo, during* **MARILYN***'s final hours.* **MARILYN** *responds to people she envisions. When voices answer, projected images appear on a scrim behind her.)*

*(**AT RISE**: **MARILYN**, age 36, in a creamy, silk gown is asleep on the floor. She awakes from a nightmare.)*

(Fade-in sound of a phone ringing, incessantly blurring into a buzz...)

MARILYN. *(terrified, calls out)* What's that? Who's here?

(clanking of a metal door closing)

My eyes are swollen. I can't breathe.

(snapping of a bolt lock)

Oh! *(frustrated, humor)* Did I do myself in?

(grating like a prisoner walking in ball and chains)

– Take too many pills? *(jokingly:)* I tried suicide once; it didn't work.

(more heavy footsteps)

Hello! *(baffled)* Where am I? New York? L.A.?

(She frets about this. Self-important.) My house is on a cul-de-sac! No one will find me.

(swooshing sound of air shooting over the floor)

(panicked) Who's that? *(screams)* Somebody!

(We hear a labored breathing.)

(forceful) I'm not finished. This isn't the end of me.

(terrified) I'm shaking. Is it night sweats? Too many pills.

(shrieks) Anybody here! Who's in my house.

*(Behind her in the dimness we see Marilyn's house, 5
Helena Drive, on a small street, almost like an alley.)*

Scene Two

(Lapse of time of only a few moments.)

OFFSTAGE VOICE. You're at the crossroads.

MARILYN. *(reaching heavenward)* Someone's getting inside my body. *(terrified)* Who are you? Are you trapped too?

OFFSTAGE VOICE (AGENT). Your agent.

MARILYN. *(angry)* You're not my – Johnny Hyde. I went to your funeral.

An old man was in the casket.

OFFSTAGE VOICE. *(voice echoes/fades)* I'm the voice he speaks through.

MARILYN. Johnny, come back! I'm barely breathing. Get a clinic to revive me. Private doctor. No publicity.

(spreads her arms, rises)

Oh my god. *(flabbergasted)* I'm floating over the scene, up 30 feet.

(looks down, horrified)

I see myself lying on my side in a fetal position. It's quiet.

(A marquee appears projected on the scrim. Perhaps one with blinking lights.)

(scared) There's a sign!

(She grabs her glasses, pushes them back on her nose. Reads the sign:) "Heaven is a Hollywood set filmed by unseen cameras.

You must audition to get through those Golden Gates. There will be signs along the way to instruct you."

(removes her glasses, putting then aside)

What the – *(throwing a tantrum)* Johnny! Where are you? I can't die now – and if I did, why would I audition for – ?

(Pushing on her glasses. Reads another sign) "Complex lives need a final review.

MARILYN. *(cont.)* You must bare your soul.

Not hide behind makeup, wigs, props."

(rebellious) I'm not dying!

(defiant) I'm studying Freud. Training with Lee. I'm still in shape!

I run, inspect my body for wrinkles, for age spots!

(Another marquee beams projected on the scrim.)

(She fumbles on her glasses. Reads the sign:)

"You can do a three minute scene from *The Misfits.* It's your last picture and you should know the lines."

(disgusted, whipping off the glasses)

Do I have to? Where's my agent? Shouldn't he be the authority.

(Waits irritated. Shoves on the glasses. Reads:)

"He says *Misfits* was your best picture."

(perturbed over the glasses) I've more to express than that role permitted.

(reads) "There was no porn in that picture and without a good clean audition, you'll go to hell."

(self-important) What if I don't choose to die? *(deathly pause)* Fine, I don't decide that. Okay. What are the rules?

(reads annoyed) "You have 15 minutes to prepare while your agent finds a scene partner."

Look, I need a living audience to find me, to complete my form.

(reads) "You may use the time to go over your scene or say goodbye to three people. Choose!"

(throwing down the glasses) I don't know!

(demanding) Why are you hiding behind all these signs?

(On the scrim, we see fleeting pictures of old actresses and movie stars.)

OFFSTAGE VOICE (AGENT). *(off)* Garbo retired at 36. Baby Jean Harlow, died at 26. You'll become a legend.

MARILYN. *(imperious)* I can't die now. I know all about Baby Jean Harlow. She wouldn't leave home without looking at her "lucky mirror." Bill Powell – bought three crypts at Forest Lawn. For Harlow, her mom, and himself.

(dismissive) Harlow and Garbo were sex goddesses. *(pause)* I'm more than that.

(proud) I'm becoming a serious actress. I not only want to be good; I have to be.

Acting is my way to grow and fix things.

I was an angry person before – the world around me was grim –

When acting, I can become my own mother. Make the world whole again.

Speak like I'm not worried about anything. Sound like a real person talking.

Characters are there. Always there. Permanently there. A script is my lifeline.

If I wasn't an actress, I don't know what I'd call myself.

(flabbergasted) Do you even know what I do onstage? I break down each scene into beats – that's Russian for "bits."

(Another marquee pops on.)

(Fumbles on her glasses. Reads:) "Choose what you'll do with your last 15 minutes."

(throwing a tantrum) I'm thinking. Look, I don't like your proposal.

(desperate) Let me go back. I've got ten more good years – I'll weigh my actions with greater care. Keep my ways virtuous and simple.

OFFSTAGE VOICE (AGENT). You were never virtuous.

MARILYN. Right…You men made the conditions of my hire. I had to do awful things just to get an interview.

But I didn't marry *you* because I didn't love you. You were too old.

The real actress was me looking like I wanted YOU in bed.

OFFSTAGE VOICE (AGENT). Can the pity party. *(pause)* I got them to put your lines on the wall.

MARILYN. *(irritated)* I didn't say I'd use this fifteen minutes to work on my scene. I might want to go back.

OFFSTAGE VOICE (AGENT). Better fix up. Use a comb, rouge, lipstick.

MARILYN. *(vicious)* You're an awful agent. Cold as a lizard and sly – .

Forced me to show off my girlhood!

Take pills and screw my head off and think I was a free spirit.

Put mirrors on my walls, and tables so I could scrutinize every angle.

(pause) Be sure I had flawless skin, heavy lidded eyes, bright red lips.

*(**MARILYN** pivots before full mirrors.)*

Are all these mirrors part of the audition?

Look, I didn't say I wanted to use the time to prepare. I'm thinking I want to go back.

(mad) I don't believe one self lasts a lifetime.

I need to mature as an actor. I'm a businesswoman. I have my own company.

Still, standing by the mirror I greet "age:" tiny crow's feet, stretch marks,

(lifts her hands) pale brown spots. My skin is pasty, my hair is fried.

(clutches her chest) My breasts are flabby. Cut them off!

(rips off her skirt to show her abdominal scar) I can't wear a bikini.

I'm like a bit of mercury. I press here and I squirt out there.

That gall bladder operation ruined my side.

I can't change my image!

(riled) I know my hair's fried: my skin's pasty.

I was losing weight using amphetamines and cigarettes.

MARILYN. *(cont.)* *(laughs, vexed)* I'd hoped to rally from this overdose and wear sparkles to work!

(Collapses in frustration. Looks up slowly. She sees her deathbed.)

Oh no, down the hall, there's my housekeeper and the doctor. I know why they're crying.

(fade-in: a rushing sound like a tornado)

I'm a brain and eyes. I have no body. Here in space, I'm nothing but mind.

(Another marquee appears.)

(Pushes on her glasses. Reads:) The Misfits.

(maddened) I didn't say I'd use these last minutes to prepare my scene.

I want to go back. *Visit three people*, while my scene partner is found.

(exasperated) Am I definitely dying? Is there's no hope.

OFFSTAGE VOICE (TRAIN ANNOUNCER). There is always hope for you, Marilyn, if people want you enough.

MARILYN. Who are you?? *(No one answers.)* All these voices! I'm so confused.

(fade-in sound of siren and voices)

(Again she sees her deathbed.)

Oh no. I see the ambulance coming and people trying to get me out of bed. *(urgent, provoked)* Can't they pump my stomach?

(fade-in: sound of slow heartbeat)

OFFSTAGE VOICE (TRAIN ANNOUNCER). During the last 15 minutes, the power of love could DRAW YOU BACK. If not, you'll have to *audition cold*. They'll be no rehearsals, no preparation.

(fade-out sound of heartbeat)

MARILYN. *(a long cry)* Joe!

(lights shift)

Scene Three

(Lapse of time of only a few moments.)

(fade-in sound of a man breathing)

MARILYN. *(cont.)* Joe. Where are you? *(blinks her eyes, anxious)* I blink. You appear there. *(blinks again)* and there. *(startled)* I can think you anywhere.

(ecstatic) You're my white knight. Stardust created many times over.

Every time I look at you – I see the sun, power, thrills.

My eyelashes go up and down and little stars come out of me.

Oh, Joe. You haven't heard from me for a few days... because

I'm here with all these ghosts!

I'm sure to end up dead if I do what they say.

(fade-in sound of a ticking clock)

Call me back into my body. I went out through some opening.

(demanding) Find a doctor. Pump my stomach

I know life has to be savored. Enjoyed fully.

(proudly) I want to return to play Chekhov, Ibsen, Somerset Maugham.

(We hear the sounds of a couple shouting at each other and a man yelling.)

(uptight) Don't you like that?

(Looks down, alarmed. Again she sees her deathbed.)

I see my body and the emergency crew.

They're shooting me with something, putting a paddle to my chest.

(panicked) A stern doctor, nurse and strangers stand by.

(MARILYN *is losing hold on reality. Her body is starting to disconnect.)*

MARILYN. *(cont.)* Somehow I can't reach you. I'm underwater.

I talk, but you can't hear me…Joe!!

(She begins to shake.) Oh no, I'm going into your body.

I see and hear with your eyes and ears.

(anguished) I'm can't cope with the–

I hurt you when I acted, but you wanted to love me.

I feel your warmth trying to help me be a GOOD WIFE.

(She comes out of his body.)

(spooked) Your kindness scared me, so I couldn't accept it.

…My shrink says I'm too male in my ambition.

Forgive me.

(guilt-stricken) In reality, I'm one window in your house. You've a lot of other windows.

(fade-in sound of lapping waves)

(confused) Oops, I'm outside my body again.

Who am I if I can go in and out of Joe's mind? Then pop back inside myself.

(sees her deathbed)

(keyed up) I know I'm in trouble.

The nurse looks scared. The doctor's left. I'm alone down there.

OFFSTAGE VOICE (CORONER). We can't get a pulse! We've lost her. She's gone.

MARILYN. I'm outside my head. I can't move it from side to side.

I've slipped totally off my body, like a glove.

(light changes)

Scene Four

(Lapse of time of only a few seconds. **MARILYN** *looks up transfixed. On the scrim appear beautiful clouds and sky.)*

MARILYN. *(cont.)* Is that heaven? I took one peek at the sky, and everything sort of appeared.

The golden gates look gracious.

Having been raised near Paramount, I want to live amongst the buildings for a while.

(fade-up of music)

Wonderful Music.

(A blinking marquee slides on.)

(She pushes on her glasses.)

(reads) "You have had a glimpse of heaven.

– As we get closer to heaven, Music will increase."

OFFSTAGE VOICE (STAGE MANAGER). *(off)* Ten minutes to your audition, Marilyn.

MARILYN. I want to see…Mama!

*(****MARILYN***'s arms lift like wings.)*

Oops. I say something and I fly. I'm a fairy.

(looks below, horrified) What are those dark buildings.

(Pause. Pushes down her fear) "Norwalk State Institution."

(shocked) I fly through a door.

(sniffs) What's this smell? Lysol?

(gags) Don't they air the room? Change the sheets? *(to self)* Leave!

(looks up, terrified) Mommie!

(pause, grief-struck) It's Norma Je–, Je–, ane…Make a sound if you know I'm here.

(Hears gasping sound. Moves closer to hug her mother, stops shocked.)

I can't kiss your face. My lips are only images.

(Sound of a loudspeaker: "Visiting hours end in five minutes.")

MARILYN. *(cont.)* This is the last time I'll see you alive.

We can't live off my beauty, anymore. It can't feed us pure oxygen.

(sound of footsteps and door opening)

No. I can't change your bedpan or wash you!

(buzzing sound)

Don't call the nurse. I repeat. Everything in my body is leaving. –

Without me there'll be no one to pay for –

Don't ring that bell. I'm going to have to put you to sleep and take you with me.

(sounds of distributing trays)

I can't feed you. Change your –

(Loudspeaker, "Visiting hours will end in three minutes.")

OFFSTAGE VOICE (AGENT). Sell Mom on death.

MARILYN. You weren't the mom I wanted.

I wanted a mom who WONDERED me!

– who said sweet things and bought me pale pink underwear.

A mom whose reason for living was to bring beauty to ME.

Who touched my hand and felt my whole being.

Do you know what it is like to always be wanting your mother. MOM!

Give me back my SOMETHING *(words slur)* I DON'T KNOW WHAT YOU TOOK FROM ME BUT I WANT IT BACK.

(We move into Marilyn's fantasy.)

*(**MARILYN** mixes a pill of poison in her mother's water.)*

MARILYN. *(cont.)* *(to her mother:)* I'm going to put something in your drink to bring you along. Swallow it!

(Loudspeaker, "Visiting hours are over.")

OFFSTAGE VOICE (MOM). MY BABY GIRL …

MARILYN. *(to her mother:)* DON'T SWALLOW THAT!

OFFSTAGE VOICE (MOM). *(echo-like)* BA-BY …

MARILYN. *(to agent)* I can't kill her even though she DEFILED me.

(sound of a ticking clock)

(panicked) MOM'S vanished…Am I saved?

I don't want to go back to dying!

(fanning her cheeks, frustrated) I'm hot.

Am I in Hell? My thermostat is totally broken. I'm never at peace.

(lights shift)

(sound of a gurney clanking)

Scene Five

(No lapse of time. She looks up, horrified, at a vision of her corpse.)

MARILYN. *(cont.)* Who's on that gurney? I can see through the sheet. That's me.

Don't take me to the MORGUE.

Some people DO come back from the dead!

OFFSTAGE VOICE (AGENT). Call Arthur.

MARILYN. *(nervous)* I can't talk to him. It's not what I say it's WHO he is.

He was the first artist/genius who RAISED ME UP!

I cheated and Arthur took me back every week for five years. Bobby and Jack Kennedy, Peter Lawford, Richard Burton, Elia Kazan, Marlon Brando, Yves Montand...

Can none of my lovers help me?

OFFSTAGE VOICE (AGENT). *(echo-like)* A-r-t-h-u-r!

MARILYN. Glimmers of stability...

OFFSTAGE VOICE (AGENT). *(echo-like)* A-r-t-h-u-r!

MARILYN. Even they went over time.

(sound of tolling bells)

What's that sound?

(lights shift)

Scene Six

(Lapse of a few moments. **MARILYN** *sees in front of her a study, a bedroom, but can't hold on to the image.)*

(She is losing her grounding in reality.)

(a swooshing sound)

MARILYN. *(with dread)* Arthur's somewhere room –
(perturbed, walks closer) My god. He's thinner than I recall. Life whittled him away.

(Sound of a man snoring. It's Arthur.)

(To Arthur:) It's Marilyn. I'm dying, honey, but I can't let go of my yearning and attachment to you.

(sound of a man breathing)

You're fast asleep. I can't touch you.
I seem to be in some body, although it's not physical.
I have arms and a shape like a cloud of colors.
Wake up. Bring me back or help me *die.* I want to pass peacefully.

(sound of rain)

Another bad rain. *(fearfully)* I'll decompose faster.
Oh, Arthur. You are the last one who can help me. I want to act again.
I'm greedy to make art!
(jokes, self-important) I also want to be *blown up* on the big screen so I'll never be ignored.
It'll be dawn soon. Light vanishes me. I can't be judged now.

(rain falls)

Awful rain! I didn't take the time to close off the angers. I followed the mirror.
(holds up a mirror) And now I can't see myself in it.
I wasn't afraid of death because I wasn't thinking of it.

MARILYN. *(cont.)* Arthur! Don't get up. Light disappears me!

(alarm keeps droning)

I've begun looking at the most important things in my life.

The biggest problem for *us* was *me.*

(rain falls harder)

(to agent) I'm dissolving, Johnny.

Oh, Arthur. My life was filled with distractions, then I just became older, and there's nothing to show my real talent.

(phone rings)

Don't get that.

(angry) Death was very much alive in you, Arthur. You lived the rising in the rising. Saw everything as it is.

I was like a peacock. So ashamed when someone pulled my feathers, I hid myself.

Don't let me die tortured. Tell me what to do!

(baffled) In case I have to pass.

Your lips moving, but I can't hear you.

Maybe it's the rain. Maybe I'm deaf.

What's that you say? "Read poetry." Try harder. Talk louder.

OFFSTAGE VOICE (ARTHUR). *(echoes)* Poetry helps face the grave.

(Lights flash on a tiny golden poetry book. She grasps it but it falls.)

MARILYN. I can't hold the book.

(sound of a ticking clock)

Arthur, you're disappearing! Don't go!

(picks up the poetry book)

Oh, now I can pick the book up.

(astonished) Sometimes my hands work. Sometimes they don't.

(She skims through the book.)

(On the scrim we see the words in red.)

(She shoves on her glasses, reads.)

MARILYN. *(cont.)* "My Captain does not answer,
his lips are pale and still,
My father does not feel my arm,
he has no pulse nor will."
I suppose Whitman is my favorite poet. But how can
he help me?

(scrutinizes a margin) What's this note in Arthur's hand?

(Projected on the scrim, we see a scribble.)

(reads, flabbergasted) "Marilyn has no acting talent. How
could she have fooled me?"

(throws book down)

(She goes to a window.)

(cowers) Is that street construction? I can't see through
the rain gusts.

(She sees her corpse.)

(horrified) No. That's me. I can see through the casket
lid.
They're taking my body to the Hall of Memories! Crypt
24.
My god, I've died.

(She collapses on a chair. Looks up, staggered.)

(baiting) Is there no sign now? I was a Christian
Scientist then a good Jew.

(imperious) Can't you get a rabbi to pray over–
Is there no assistance?

(MARILYN *glances about. Spies the golden book, anx-
iously opens it.)*

*(Behind her, on the scrim, we see projected words as she
bobbles on her glasses. Reads.)*

MARILYN. *(cont.)* Emily Dickinson said:

"Because I could not stop for Death,
He kindly stopped for me;
The carriage held but just ourselves
And immortality."

(pause, holding back tears)

"We slowly drove, he knew no haste,
And I had put away
My labor, and my leisure too,
For his civility."

(pause, forces herself on)

"We passed the school, where children strove
At recess, in the ring:
We passed the fields of gazing grain,
We passed the setting sun."

(light changes)

Scene Seven

(Lapse of a few moments. We see a gold-rimmed rising sun. We hear music of a soprano singing a cappella.)

MARILYN. *(cont.)* Lovely Music!

(Shoves on her glasses. Reads a sign:) "You are now officially dead.

– To get into Heaven, you must audition with a scene, a song, and an interview."

"If you pass the scene audition, you will proceed to the Music audition and the interview."

(yells) No more visits? Mercy!

(A streak of light.)

(mystified) Whose arm is that shooting out the sky, grabbing me?

Tubes of light run up his hands. *(astonished)* It's CLARK GABLE!

Clark, darling! Everything you do is strange and exciting –

OFFSTAGE VOICE (GABLE). I'm your scene partner. The lines are on that wall.

OFFSTAGE VOICE (GHOSTS AND WIND). Marilyn. Is that… Marilyn! Monroe. Act for us!!

MARILYN. *(to ghosts)* Leave!

(to Clark, aggravated) I can't do *The Misfits*!!

Oh, Clark. I cried every day the month you died.

– That was the first time I realized you weren't God.

(disgusted) You didn't die from…me!

You were drinking and smoking three packs a day!

Arthur's script was weak. Scenes ranged from bad to tolerable.

The words were – . I couldn't do them.

(cries out) You were bound to get tired of waiting for me.

Women weren't meant to be hunters. We're not good at it.

And men who treat us *like equals* get confused.

MARILYN. *(cont.)* I tried. Up at midnight running lines.
Gulping Nembutal, even pricking the capsules for
faster effect.

(laughs, miffed) Was I getting even for the years Dad
never showed up?

Oh no! You're fading *(cries) Stay!* We could read from
these –

(searches through her poetry book)

I do better with fresh material!

(looks up, glum) Clark's gone.

(A marquee appears.)

(Struggles with her glasses. Reads) "Your scene partner's
left.

– From now on, you must audition alone."

(to self, sarcastic) Surprise. Surprise.

(Another marquee appears.)

(annoyed, reads) "Why not read a poem? Try Auden."

(Fade-up light on book. She scans the poem.)

(Music: Echoes of Children's Music Box Sounds)

*(A marquee appears with the words, "Audition Scene:
Read this Elegy." She reads, disgusted:)*

"But for her it was her
Last afternoon as herself.
An afternoon of nurses and rumours…
The current of her feeling failed
she became her admirers."

(throwing aside her glasses) I don't want to act out a *death*
poem.

When I'm not thinking of death, I'm not afraid.

Can any poem express how *sorry* I feel. *Ashamed* that
I've nothing to say!

Scene Eight

(There is no lapse of time. Just the sound of wild applause.)

OFFSTAGE VOICE (STANISLAVSKI). *(Russian accent)* I approve. You have passed the scene audition. You may proceed to your interview, Norma Jeane.

MARILYN. But I was – Who are you?

OFFSTAGE VOICE (STANISLAVSKI). Stanislavski.

MARILYN. *(breathless)* You're not…the great Russian master!!! *(falls on her knees)* Then I'll respectfully correct you.

I'm Marilyn Monroe. I use my mom's maiden name.

(looks about) Appear, please! I need to stare into your soul.

(spots him, gasps) Mr. Stanislavski! Waive my audition.

I followed your rules. Kept a Russian coach. Used emotional recall.

God knows how many times I killed Maf, my dog.

I was always your devotee. Hiding with my script to score my lines.

Studying your books because all the dumb models died tragically and unknown.

Maybe if I hadn't read them, I wouldn't feel so…so stupid.

Actors rehearsed for years in Moscow – They didn't do interviews!

OFFSTAGE VOICE (AGENT). Ordinary English baffles Stanislavski. He's gone.

MARILYN. No. *(calls out, anxious)* Mr. Stanislavski!

(She paces as a metronome clicks.)

Where are the dead poets? Appear, cowards!

I'm losing everything, my house, my relationships, my body, my mind.

(A marquee lights up on the screen.)

(She put on her glasses uncertainly.)

MARILYN. *(cont.)* *(reads)* "We don't have to show up; we're God. You are officially dead."

(Revolted, she reads on.) "And, death once dead, there's no more dying then."

(fed up) How can I feel so alive and be so dead?

(Another marquee appears.)

An obituary? "August 4, 1962: Marilyn Monroe found dead with an empty bottle of barbiturates.

– Her fame as a sex goddess outshone her acting talent."

I can't be *remembered* like –

OFFSTAGE VOICE (AGENT). Pass into a higher plane –

MARILYN. I can scarcely think of my career without weeping.

OFFSTAGE VOICE (AGENT). And you'll be rediscovered on earth.

(Sound of street noise fades into dreamy violin Music, Ravel, Daphnis et Cloe.)

Scene Nine

(Lapse of a few seconds. She looks up fumbles on her glasses, frustrated.)

MARILYN. *(cont.)* "Part two: the music audition. You have fifteen minutes."

(sound of heavy piano Music intrudes)

"You will be given 2 songs and one dance piece. We are looking for actors that move.
– First song is 'Happy Birthday!'"

(to self) Oh yes, they do that at the Lee's Studio.

(She hums a Happy Birthday song. A siren goes off.)

Oh no! What's that screeching –

(She pushes glasses back on her nose. Reads sign:)

"You have insulted our President. You could go to hell. Pick another song."
But I knew him before. *(hollers)* Turn that up!
I don't want to audition anymore.

(Lights flash on and off.)

I don't want to go further.
I'm moving toward some sort of audition at the end of the tunnel.

(Stage lights grow larger and larger.)

Turn down the lights. I can't see where my accompanist is.

(Sound: Music explodes about her.)

MARILYN. *(cont.)* Look let me sing from something I know.

(Another alarm goes off.)

What the…is – that?

(Shoves on her glasses, exasperated.)

"You may pick your own song."
Thank God!

MARILYN. *(cont.) (reads on)* "But you must do an interpretive dance with your song, and the movement can have no relationship to the song."

You're tough!

Fine. I'll move faster or slower than the Music.

You think I haven't hoop jumped before?

(She sings a few bars of a familiar tune. Sound: of heinous laughter.)

Don't laugh at me, jerks.

You judges hiding out in the black out there.

That number made me an icon in the U.S. of A.

OFFSTAGE VOICE (AGENT). That a girl. You tell them, baby!

(There is the sound of circles clicking black to white.)

MARILYN. Oh no. A small group of circles are ahead of me...

– making snapping sounds as they click white then black.

I can't see whose inside, but their voices are harsh.

(Sound: jeers fade in and out)

What did you say? My talent never existed?

I was allowed to imagine it? It was all a joke.

(Sound: Mocking laughter rising and falling)

How could I have made that up? This can't be eternity. Let me do my signature song.

(lights dim)

Don't dim those lights and tell me damnation is waiting. Who the hell are you!

(peers out) It's dark and immense all around, but I can do it. Give me my song!

*(**MARILYN** sings again with more passion. This time there is huge applause! Fireworks! Graffiti flowing down. Another marquee appears. She searches about for her glasses and reads, exasperated.)*

MARILYN. *(cont.)* "The second part of your interview has been approved."

How could that be? I was panned. Insulted! By some …cowards…

(pause)

No. I didn't give up on myself. That's right.

(A blinking gold marquee appears.)

"A higher power intervened."

Who judged me?

(flashing red, blue, gold, marquee)

"William Shakespeare!"

I didn't know he knew music.

He's even greater than Stanislavski!

– All these "S" men Stanislavski, Strasberg, Shakespeare believe in me!

(Bach's Keyboard Concerto No 3 in D major, BWV1054, plays.)

Scene Ten

(Lapse of a few seconds. She looks up swan-like as a marquee flashes on.)

MARILYN. *(Slips on her glasses:)* "Part three: the interview. You have fifteen minutes for three questions."

"First Question! Why do you want to act? Prove you searched for love and knowledge."

The *why* question. Makes me want to crawl under the table!

(scared, but strong) I act because I love beauty.

I want to give back. I come from love.

I view myself with each role a god with a small wand, inventing a universe.

OFFSTAGE VOICE (AGENT). 14 minutes!

MARILYN. A play is a wonderful little island for me.

The character comes with a story. I embrace her lines.

She takes hold and, I float, like a balloon…set free.

Acting is dreaming. It's my window to creation. It's everything I call god.

(A marquee blinks on.)

(She fumbles on her glasses.)

"Shouldn't you quote someone?"

(over the glasses) I don't want to hide behind somebody. That's dishonest. But, when I talk, cracks appear.

(Another marquee pops on.)

"Use Emily Dickinson. She felt like nobody, too."

(Lights up on the book. She opens it quickly.)

(recites uneasily:)

"It's all I have to bring today –
This, and my heart beside –"

OFFSTAGE VOICE (AGENT). 13 minutes!

MARILYN. "This, and my heart,
and all the fields – "

(Sound of fanfare: balloons popping, trumpets blaring, ribbons flapping.)

(A marquee flashes.)

"You've passed the first question. Meet your judges."
My, I'm rising like a silk scarf. Isn't it dreamy!

(Fade-in Music: Ravel's Daphne et Chloé)

(lights shift)

Scene Eleven

(No lapse of time. Silver forms float through a mist.)

MARILYN. Who's there? Emily? Thirteen little angels. *(plays peek a boo)* I see you.

You can't be my judges.

OFFSTAGE VOICE (AGENT). 12 minutes left.

MARILYN. Come closer, angels. Your faces shine like diamonds.

(rubs her stomach) I've lost 20 pounds!

(The sound of fluttering wings fills the stage.)

You want me to climb that spiral staircase?

I can't lift my feet.

(The room darkens. She turns about, freezing.)

(shivers) Monsoon season! Where are the little angels?

OFFSTAGE VOICE (AGENT). 11 minutes.

(sound of squealing rats)

MARILYN. I never realized how alive death is.

(shouts) You poets! Tell me what to do when the angels leave!

Some artists must – Are you trying to trick me?

OFFSTAGE VOICE (AGENT). You have 10 minutes.

MARILYN. *(screams)* Come back, angels!

(sound of trolls hissing.)

There you are. Tell me, darlings.

What's that? You're my dead babies?

(more tattling sounds)

What?! You're the *godhead. My judges.*

(A marquee lights up.)

"Second question: "How many abortions did you have?"

You're tough…I had five procedures in seven years.
I couldn't go to the gym and punch the shit out of
something.

MARILYN. *(cont.)* *(loudly)* All this back and forth with the studio, and...*crude* birth control.

Primitive rubbers. Blood clots from IUD's. Pills that got you bald, fat, or dead.

OFFSTAGE VOICE (AGENT). You have 9 minutes.

(image of a doctor's office)

MARILYN. *(sniffs)* Oh, no. I smell blood!

I'm back in time, watching studio doctors work on me. It's awful but...

I feel the way the baby and I felt when –

– I'm a ball of light screaming, no sound.

The studio sent roses, a silver platter with lunch, and a card.

"You only have the pressure of being beautiful, which you are."

OFFSTAGE VOICE (AGENT). 8 minutes to explain.

MARILYN. *(angry)* The most advertized girl in the world can't be pregnant.

When I got better the studio wrote, "Wear a hat at the beach or you'll get freckles and look like a goose egg."

OFFSTAGE VOICE (AGENT). *(off)* 7 minutes.

MARILYN. *(angry)* First time I did it, I'd a little dalliance with pills.

It wasn't a full-fledged affair.

Next time, I took a pill regularly and felt more human. After the third...Norma Jeane wanted to kill Marilyn Monroe.

(Sees an ugly slew of baby photos. She shouts as pictures flash.)

Norma loved babies but – Marilyn forced herself to act from the place she'd grown to.

She knew that tiny spec wasn't real life.

She had to ride life. Let it ride her. Let go of the steering wheel.

MARILYN. *(cont.)* Marilyn saw when not fed, these movie moguls would perch and wait for fresh meat.

(screams) "After the first death, there is no other!"

Who said that?

OFFSTAGE VOICE (AGENT). 6 minutes.

MARILYN. I lied. I had thirteen mistakes –

– I still ride on the horns of the death wish which says, "Kill it so you can act."

(A luminescence permeates everything.)

Explaining feels wonderful.

I'm racing toward a golden halo. A baby is inside it!

(Music: Schubert's Ave Maria)

OFFSTAGE VOICE (AGENT). 5 minutes.

MARILYN. *(waves)* Beauty boy. You're my best baby?

(A marquee shines on. She flounders on her glasses.)

"Third question. "Did you kill Arthur's baby?"

No. I was pregnant with Arthur three times and I carried one long enough to know I had a son.

(to baby) I was ready for you, wonder boy.

My husband was a millionaire and a genius.

Your enormous spirit stirred inside me, gluing Arthur to me.

(paces) But back-room abortions had busted my insides.

My blood pressure got higher, and the swelling went up here, through the behind.

The more I tried to hold on, the more I finally lost.

Maybe I took too many pills. But I…didn't throw myself down the basement steps.

I slipped…on…And – *after…the fall* – they took your life to save mine.

AGENT. *(off)* 4 minutes.

MARILYN. Fans sent condolences.

Arthur's baby.

Your death cut the threads between me and Arthur.

MARILYN. *(cont.)* He divorced me and turned me into a drug addict in his next play.

(looks up distraught) My baby boy's gone.

(A marquee slides on.)

"The interview's over."

OFFSTAGE VOICE (AGENT). 3 minutes to curtain.

MARILYN. But I haven't JUSTIFIED MY ACTIONS. Validated my – Did I pass –

(A rainstorm of yellow light.)

I'm rising. Forgetting everything I aimed for or wished for or thought –

(Sound of bell ringing.)

Golden gates look like Paramount! Don't close them!

OFFSTAGE VOICE (AGENT). 2 minutes to curtain.

MARILYN. Let me in – So many have come before – Beings, brighter and –

(sound of specters approaching)

GHOSTS. *(whispering)* "We are the dead/short days ago/We lived, felt dawn, saw – " [John McCrae]

*(**MARILYN** looks out at the sea of ghosts.)*

MARILYN. *(shouts to the ghosts)* Who's from California? Two or three million. We die young.

OFFSTAGE VOICE (AGENT). 1 minute to –

MARILYN. Let me stay! *(kneels, begs)* I know I did all these bad things.

OFFSTAGE VOICE (AGENT). 30 seconds to –

MARILYN. I was in a delicious whirlwind of – Stardom!! We all have these dark ambitions!

OFFSTAGE VOICE (AGENT). *(loud)* Places!

MARILYN. FORGIVE ME! *(freezes in a beam of light)* DON'T IGNORE ME.

*(as spotlight closes in on **MARILYN**'s face)*

(We hear an aria from Purcell's Dido *and* Aeneas, *Dido's Lament (When I am Laid in Earth).)*

(As stage lights go out, Marilyn's image takes over the scrim.)

End of Play

Also by
Rosary Hartel O'Neill...

Beckett at Greystones Bay

Black Jack: The Thief of Possession

Degas in New Orleans

John Singer Sargent and Madame X

A Louisiana Gentleman

Property

Solitaire

Turtle Soup

Uncle Victor

White Suits in Summer

The Wing of Madness

Wishing Aces

Please visit our website **samuelfrench.com** for complete descriptions and licensing information.

OTHER TITLES AVAILABLE FROM SAMUEL FRENCH

DEGAS IN NEW ORLEANS

Rosary Hartel O'Neill

Full Length, Drama / 3m, 6f / One integrated Interior/Exterior Set

A historical drama that explores Edgar Degas' scandalous visit to New Orleans in 1872. Edgar Degas, the French Impressionist painter, is torn between helping his relatives in America and pursuing a career as a painter. Fame and family obligations come to a head when he discovers he is still in love with his sister-in-law, who is now pregnant and blind. As Edgar struggles with his own ethical conundrum, he discovers that his aggressively charming brother has gone through all the family money in an attempt to save his uncle's sugar business.

OTHER TITLES AVAILABLE FROM SAMUEL FRENCH

BLACK JACK: THE THIEF OF POSSESSION

Rosary Hartel O'Neill

Full Length, Southern Comedy / 2m, 4f / Unit Set

Blackjack follows an eccentric Southern family as it is squeezed into the close quarters of a Mississippi cruise ship for the New Year's holiday. Kaitlyn is convinced that she is channeling the poet Baudelaire, and certain that her husband is having an affair with a larger-than-life ship entertainer. Irene, the matriarch of the family, suspects a rift in her daughter's marriage. Her sexy maid sets her sights on the grandson, a successful Southern rock star. Everyone dons costumes for New Year's Eve, casting off their old identities and trying on new loves.

OTHER TITLES AVAILABLE FROM SAMUEL FRENCH

JOHN SINGER SARGENT AND MADAME X

Rosary Hartel O'Neill

Full Length, Comedy / 5m, 4f / One integrated int/ext set.

John Singer Sargent, an up-and-coming American artist, is eager to collaborate on a portrait that would catapult him and Madame X, the most beautiful woman in Paris, to the pinnacle of society. With its revelations about Madame X's identity and an eyebrow-raising cast of characters, including Richard Wagner, Oscar Wilde, Henry James, Sarah Bernhardt, and Dr. Samuel Pozzi (Madame X's notorious gynecologist/lover), this romantic comedy exposes the tale of beauty, infatuation, obsession, and betrayal that lies behind Sargent and Madame X's masterpiece.

OTHER TITLES AVAILABLE FROM SAMUEL FRENCH

A LOUISIANA GENTLEMAN

Rosary Hartel O'Neill

Full Length, Southern Comedy / 1m, 3f / Unit Set

Blaine Ashton, a medical student in his mid-twenties from a prominent New Orleans family, has fallen in love with a middle-aged actress and is getting married, much to the chagrin of his mentally disturbed sister and his eccentric, alcoholic old Aunt. His Aunt forces him to take care of his sister after he's married and all the southern belles in the household are almost too much to bear. The histrionics never stop as the women compete for Malter's love and attention. Ultimately, an uneasy truce is called once a baby is born and Christmas rolls around, but continued craziness is undoubtedly in their future. Especially powerful roles for women.

OTHER TITLES AVAILABLE FROM SAMUEL FRENCH

THE AWAKENING OF KATE CHOPIN

Rosary Hartel O'Neill

Historical Drama / 2m, 2f

Kate Chopin, author of The Awakening, struggles to hold onto her marriage and her six small children as she launches her career as a novelist in 1884. Frustrating her attempts are: her wealthy next door neighbor, wanting to prove his masculinity; her jealous husband, stricken with malaria; the little sex-pot seamstress next door, the town gossip; and the bankrupt cotton business, which consumes all of her time. This crazy cacophony of personalities ends up compelling Kate toward her goal of becoming a famous author.